BUNION BURT

To my sweet, wonderful husband, Marc,
who loves me, sore feet and all!
—M. H.

For Johnny and Kelly
—J. E. D.

Margaret K. McElderry Books
An imprint of Simon & Schuster Children's Publishing Division
1230 Avenue of the Americas, New York, New York 10020
Text copyright © 2009 by Marsha Hayles
Illustrations copyright © 2009 by Jack E. Davis
All rights reserved, including the right of reproduction in whole or in part in any form.
Book design by Krista Vossen
The text for this book is set in Aunt Mildred.
The illustrations for this book are rendered in watercolor and acrylic.
Manufactured in China
2 4 6 8 10 9 7 5 3 1
Library of Congress Cataloging-in-Publication Data
Hayles, Marsha.
Bunion Burt / by Marsha Hayles ; illustrated by Jack E. Davis.—1st ed.
p.   cm.
Summary: Everyone from Granny Gert to Old Doctor Smurt suggests a way to make poor Burt's feet stop
hurting, but Pappy Spurt knows what Burt really needs.
ISBN: 978-1-4169-4132-3
[1. Foot—Fiction. 2. Humorous stories. 3. Stories in rhyme.] I. Davis, Jack E., ill. II. Title.
PZ8.3.H326Bun 2009
[E]—dc22   2006027520

BUNION BURT

by Marsha Hayles

illustrated by Jack E. Davis

Margaret K. McElderry Books
New York London Toronto Sydney

Bunion Burt
Had feet that hurt.
They pinched and poked and pained him.
The folks all knew
'Bout Burt's feet too—
His bunions helped nickname him.

Said Mama Myrt,
"My poor, sore Burt.
You sure got ailing tootsies.
I wish I knew
What we could do
To cure your failing footsies."

She tugged and hugged,
But Burt just shrugged—
He didn't want her fussin'.
He'd find a way
To be okay
Without so much discussin'.

So Bunion Burt
Passed up dessert
And set out for the pigsty.

There sweet sow Pert

Oinked up at Burt

To share her soothing mud pie.

Burt pinched his nose,

Then inched his toes

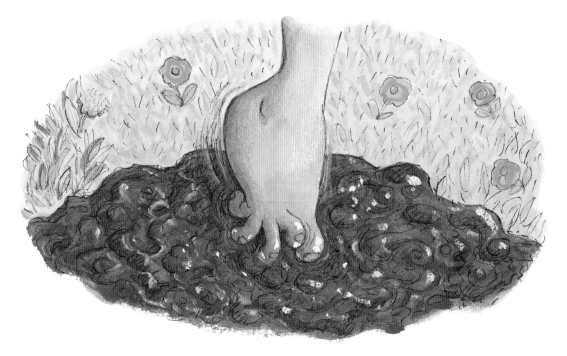

Into that juicy muck.

But Bunion Burt's
Poor feet still hurt
And STUNK when they un-STUCK!

When Granny Gert
Got whiff of Burt,
She sniffed, "You went whole hog!
Now go outside,
Get washed and dried,
And shake that stinky fog!"

Burt rubbed and scrubbed,

Out in the tub,

Then rinsed in cloudburst sprinkles.

But Bunion Burt's

Clean feet still hurt

And worse,

They now had wrinkles!

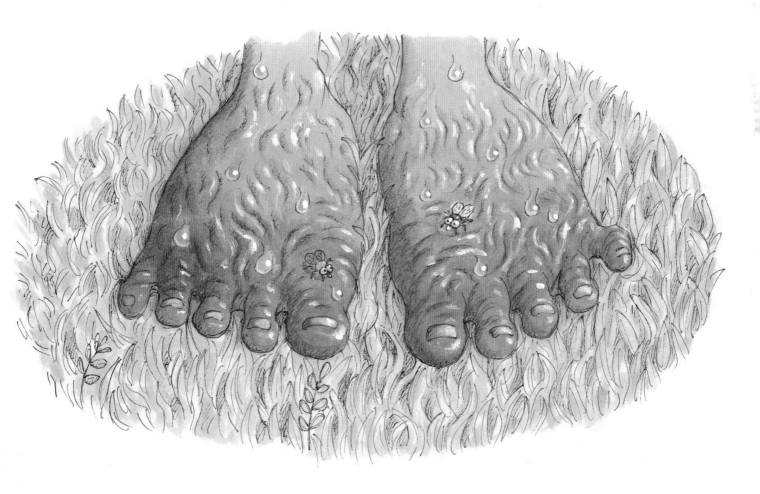

Then Cousin Kurt
Said, "Hey there, Burt.
Those feet of yours are prunes.
The rain is done.
I see the sun.
Come cook them on the dunes."

So Cousin Kurt
Took Bunion Burt
Down to the beachy shore.

Burt's pruney feet
Got red as beets.
**"THEY'RE SUNBURNED
TO THE CORE!"**

Old Doctor Smurt
Examined Burt
And said, "Your feet are fried.

Take my advice,
Put them on ice
And spend the day inside."

Burt chilled his toes
Until they froze—
They turned an icy blue.

His sister Vert

Squealed, "Really, Burt,

That color's wrong for you!"

"I'll paint your toes
A bright red rose
And buff them till they shine.

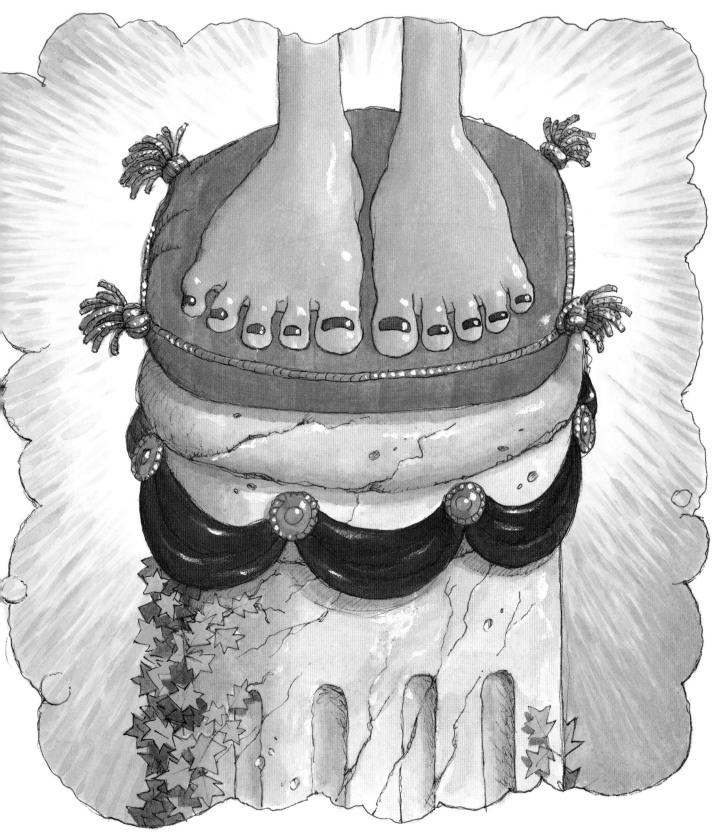

I know for sure
My pedicure
Will make your feet divine!"

With that, Burt burst,

"This is the WORST— I'm BEAT from being treated."

He wailed,
"I'm NAILED.
All cures
have FAILED.
My feet have me
DEFEATED!"

Said Pappy Spurt
To achin' Burt,
"You stop your weep 'n' woe-in'.
Your feet are fine,
They're big like mine—
They just keep on a-growin'.
We'll get some pep
Back in your step
And bring you up to speed.
No need to feel
Like one big heel—
I know just what you need."

Soon Bunion Burt
Called Mama Myrt
And sweet sow Pert
And Granny Gert
And Cousin Kurt
And Old Doc Smurt
And Sister Vert
And, most of all,
His pappy Spurt,
And said he had some news—

"I'M BIGFOOT BURT! MY FEET DON'T HURT!"

"THEY'RE CURED BY
MY NEW SHOES!"